MINE!

by
RACHEL
BRIGHT

PUFFIN

Allow me to introduce you to **Fifi**

and **Frankie**

....the
twins.

Fifi's **best** things are ponies,

princesses and the colour pink.

Her **worst** thing is peas.

Frankie's **best** things are
bears,
bicycling
and the
colour blue.

Her **worst**
thing is bedtime.

But they both have the same
bestest thing in the

whole

wide

world...

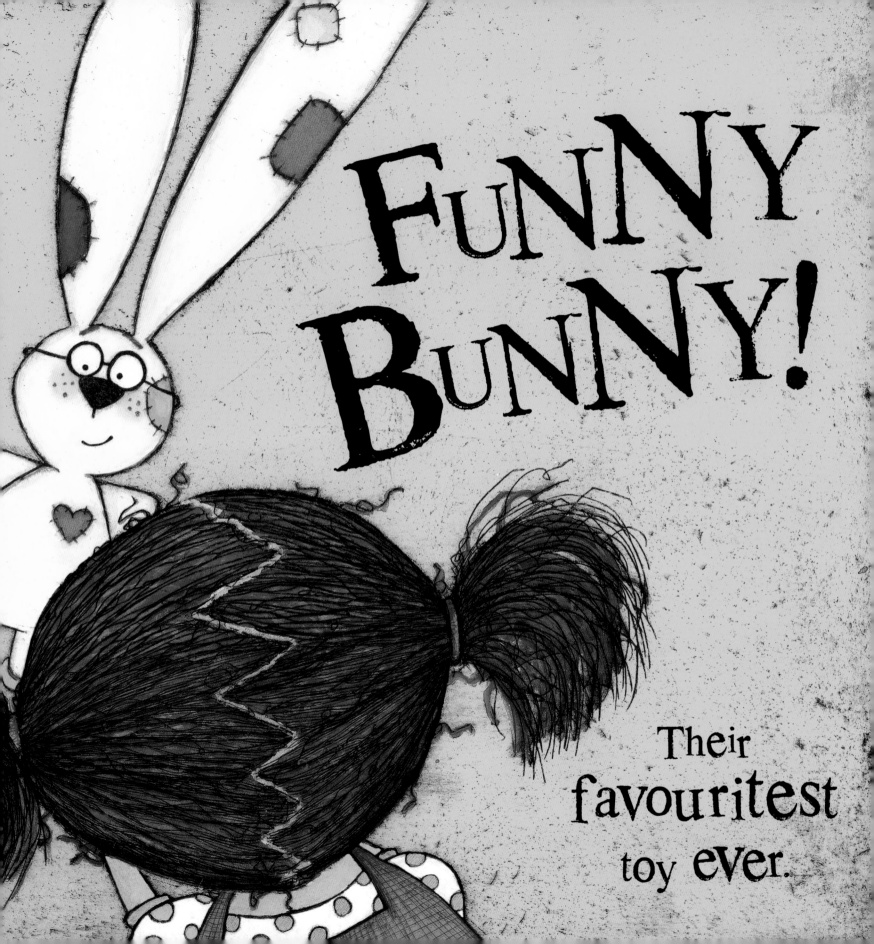

FUNNY BUNNY!

Their favouritest toy ever.

Fifi loves to dress him up in pink.

(not blue)

very girly dress →

↑ fifi's pants
very special
rabbit hat

Frankie loves to take him on the **teddy-bear express.**

(no ponies allowed)

Wherever the twins go, Funny Bunny goes too.
Today they are visiting Grandma Flo.

"I'm holding
Funny Bunny."
Fifi **always**
wants to hold him.

"NO! I'm holding
Funny Bunny."
Frankie **always**
wants to hold him too.

But, oh dear,
you've guessed it,
there's only **One**
Funny Bunny, so . . .

"But he's MINE!" wails Fifi. "Gimme

"No, he's MINE!" cries Frankie

And... they...

puuuuuullllll

"...You BROKE Funny Bunny!"

AAAAAAAAAAA!
WAAAAAAAA!
WAAAAAAAA!
WAAAAAAAAA!
WAAAAAAAAA!

Funny Bunny couldn't believe
his not-there-any-more ears.

WA.

No, yoU BROKE FunnY Bunny!"

WAAAAAA

WAAAAA

A! WAA WAAAA

WAAAA

And neither could
Grandma Flo.

It was definitely
time to explain that
sometimes
you have to **share**.

And so, while Grandma Flo mended
Funny Bunny one ear at a time,
they worked something
out **together**.

And now on Mondays

and wednesdays

and **Fridays**, it's Fifi's turn to play with **Funny Bunny**.

Which is **ok** with **Frankie**, because on **Tuesdays**

and

Thursdays

and **Saturdays**, it's her turn to play with him.

And even though sharing isn't always easy . . .

...everybody

loves Sundays!

well...

...almost everybody.

For my lovely grandmas & incredible grandads, with all my never-ending love

And with ginormous thank-yous to Robbie & Elvis for unwavering loveliness & to the fabulously talented Mandy & Rebecca & Goldy.

PUFFIN BOOKS
Published by the Penguin Group: London, New York, Australia,
Canada, India, Ireland, New Zealand and South Africa
Penguin Books Ltd, Registered Offices:
80 Strand, London WC2R 0RL, England

puffinbooks.com

First published 2011
006
Made and printed in China
ISBN: 9780241379073

In loving memory of Leningrad (small cuddly dog) –
my favouritest toy ever . . . lost on a beach
(in Wales c. 1981) but not forgotten.